"Ron Kolm's sub-Homeric comedy of ill-manners, *Duke & Jill*, expounds in twelve sharply pointed chapters, the misadventures of a heinous couple you might have encountered if you lived on the Lower East Side in the 70s and 80s. A few of these calcified Dukes and shriveled Jills still hobble around the neighborhood today, perambulating slowly from methadone clinic to park bench, unregenerate degenerates who can't even remember what it was they did wrong. Kolm's minimal prose limns these larcenous lowlifes with a regard that's almost tender. Almost." —**Max Blagg**, author of *Pink Instrument* and *Ticket Out*.

"The old New York of the 1980s comes alive in this series of plaintive tales featuring the anti-heroic middle-aged survivalists, Duke and Jill. Ron Kolm's writing is delicate, empathetic, deadpan, and places the reader in the center of the action, where nothing and everything is happening at the same time. His point of view is never voyeuristic, but more like a comrade, living out his life alongside his characters. His stories never turn out the way you imagine, and then they do." —**Lewis Warsh**, author of *One Foot Out The Door: The Collected Stories of Lewis Warsh* and *Inseparable*.

"If you're roaming the East Village today and lived there before NYU bought it out, you might need a map to recognize where you are—it looks nothing like what it used to. Ron Kolm's *Duke & Jill* builds a kind of holograph map of the EV streets, shops, and characters of those bygone days. Drug-riddled dreamers, Duke and Jill tumble through misadventures that flower and crumble much like Calvino's Marcovaldo schemes: doomed to the harsh bourgeois soils to which the neighborhood has succumbed. Kolm's rhythmic, no-nonsense style deserves a standing ovation for its clean reconstruction of the enclave where fairy-rings danced nightly before they cooked themselves to a crisp and the dragons of real-estate swallowed them whole ..." —**Susan Brennan**, author of *numinous, Verse* (a web series) and director of the feature film *Vegas*.

"These stories bring tears to my eyes and laughter to my lips. Old Testament East Village, so many classic moments that now seem lost to time. Kolm's short tales of Duke and Jill start out innocently enough, yet pack truthful punches in their amusing finales. He has captured the details and characters of the old neighborhood far more effectively in these few pages than an entire shelf of books that have been written about the area since then." —**Arthur Nersesian**, author of *the Fuck-Up* and *Manhattan Loverboy*.

DUKE

& JILL

RON KOLM

Copyright © 2015 by RON KOLM

PUBLISHED BY UNKNOWN PRESS

First Edition

ISBN: 978-0-9963526-1-1

edited by Bud Smith
cover by Jeffrey Isaac
back cover portrait by Bob Witz
illustrations by Dan Freeman, Bill Anthony, Daniel Kolm, Gregory Kolm, Shalom Neuman and Fly
book design by Bud Smith

www.unknowneverything.com

Some of these stories have appeared in the following anthologies: *Between C & D* (the magazine and the Penguin paperback), *A Day in the Life* and *Help Yourself!* (both published by Autonomedia), *Have A NYC 2* and *Have A NYC 3* (Three Rooms Press) and *Too Much: Tales of Excess* (Unknown Press). Individual stories appeared in the following magazines: The Gary Indiana issue of *New Observations, Beet, Redtape, DUMB, MungBeing, Instant Classics, Public Illumination Magazine, Appearances*, the *Hobo Camp Review*, and *The Disagreement*.

'Bad Karma' was turned into a film that was directed by Jim Spring. It is archived at the New Museum in NYC: (https://archive.org/details/XFR_2013-08-31_2B_03).

CONTENTS

For Michael Lindgren, with gratitude

WHEN THE LOWER EAST SIDE WAS ON FIRE

Bud Smith

I MOVED FROM NEW JERSEY to New York City in 2007. I was working at a power plant in Jersey City, NJ, at the time, welding a new roof on the boiler. One of my co-workers asked me, "What street you live on now?"

"173rd street."

"And what?" Meaning the intersection.

"Haven Avenue."

"Oh I know exactly where that is, right on the river, view of the bridge."

This surprised me. The guy was older and to my knowledge wouldn't have much to say about the neighborhood I'd just moved into. But I was wrong, as kids are often wrong.

He said, "I used to drive my Valiant there to go buy coke. What's the address of your building?"

"138."

"Huh," he thought for a minute. "Sounds 'bout right. Be careful, your street is a perfect place to get shot, stabbed or high."

But by the time I got here, New York City was different. My co-worker was remembering a time that's gone, vanished—poof. The city has been cleaned up. Been scrubbed clean. He was thinking about the time when he could drive across the GWB and score coke out in the open. I didn't mention that my street now has a Starbucks on it. My street has a college campus for medical students (who don't know how to party) (trust me, I've tried.)

In 2011, I ran into Ron Kolm at a reading near Union Square. I'd been here in New York long enough to know my way around and feel at home. Ron read a poem about being attacked by a vagrant in a NYC bookstore, being stabbed through the hand, chasing the person out of the store with his bloody hand.

I had to talk to Ron. "That poem true?"

He held up his hand and showed me the scar.

We got to talking more and more about how New York has changed over the years (as any city will do). We got to talking and as usually happens, the past of NYC came up. Specifically the 70s and 80s, when punk reigned supreme. When an artist could live in the East Village and afford to do so. When things were gleefully dangerous.

"The Lower East Side was on fire," Ron said.

Which to me, I initially took as

meaning, it was hip. It was the place to be.

But no. Ron actually meant: "It was on fucking fire! I was working at Eastside Bookstore and I used to go out and watch buildings burn. You know all those little green spots, the little parks? They used to be buildings at one time that burnt down. Junkies would fall asleep in bed with cigarettes. Everything burned ..."

Ron Kolm's *Duke & Jill* stories are heaven to me. I read them with the same sense of discovery that a small child might have when reading *The Wizard of Oz*. Here's this place that's described, full of these people that are gone. Most of them anyway. They can't afford to live in New York City anymore. There's no apartments full of punk rockers on the island of Manhattan that I know of. People have been pushed out to the furthest reaches of the city: Washington Heights (me), Queens, Brooklyn, even Jersey City, New Jersey.

But here, in the land of make believe, Duke and Jill live in, it's still that time when deadbeat kids full of blood and wonder live and play and fuck on the lower east side of Manhattan, no one wants it yet—it's on fire.

DUKE & JILL

Dan Freeman

DUKE AND JILL

DUKE AND JILL DO DRUGS. They live on the corner of Avenue A and 10th Street, in a mostly burnt-out building. Duke is originally from Wisconsin. Jill is from Wisconsin, too. They don't have much else in common.

Bad things keep happening to them. Their best friend, a junky, rents a truck, backs it up over the curb, kicks in their apartment door, and takes all their stuff. The TV, the stereo, even their beat-up sofa. He knows they'll be out, getting loaded in a neighborhood bar, trying to score some coke. In fact, they're waiting for him to show up with some reasonable blow.

Duke is pissed. He buys a gun, a .38 caliber, used, but still workable, from a guy he knows on the street. Duke and Jill don't fight much the next couple of weeks—she doesn't trust him not to shoot her if the going gets too hot. So things chill out for a while.

One night Duke is sitting around getting loaded. In that condition he hears a banging on the hastily repaired door. He gets his gun and tucks it into his belt, and opens the door, unbolting a newly installed double-bar police lock.

The guy at the door turns out to be a friend, a member of a crypto-punk band he likes a lot.

"Wow, you got a gun," the friend says.

"Yeah, but it's not loaded," Duke replies. He points the gun at the ceiling and pulls the trigger. The hammer clicks. "I just keep it around to scare Jill

—keep her in line," he laughs. "Actually, I got it to blow away the scumbag who stole our stuff. If I ever see his ass in the neighborhood he's gone."

"Man, let me see that thing," his friend says, excited by the unusual toy. He points the gun at a boarded up window and pulls the trigger. The hammer clicks again. He giggles and aims the gun at his temple. "Deer hunter," he says, and pulls the trigger. A bright flash of orange sound bounces around the nearly empty room, stunning Duke and momentarily blinding him.

After the police leave, Jill calls all their friends to tell them the news. She has to shout to be heard above the sound of Duke vacuuming the dried blood off their shag carpet.

DUKE AND JILL HAVE A PARTY

Ron Kolm, Text   Dan Freeman, Art

The rent was going up. Someone had died in their apartment. It seemed like a good time to split.

So Duke and Jill packed their stuff and moved East. To Avenue D.

They decided to have a party to celebrate their new place. Duke bought a couple of six packs and some bags of chips, and Jill made a dip.
Duke also borrowed some tapes from a buddy. Mostly Latin-type dance music. That was about it.

They put out the word, and maybe twenty people showed up. Brought some bottles, and a generous amount of reefer. There wasn't much conversation because, really, there wasn't much to talk about. Everyone just sat around getting loaded.

Jill's old boyfriend, Arnie, was there. He kept his eye on her and, when Duke disappeared into the next room with a young thing, they got together. The party got wild. Everyone took their clothes off. Jill took pictures.

Everyone agreed that they were having a re-really good time.
So it was a real bummer when, later, the developed rolls of film got mailed to Jill's mother by mistake.

Reprinted from DUMB Magazine Vol. 17, No.3; Fall, 1996

DUKE AND JILL HAVE A PARTY

THE RENT WAS GOING UP. Someone had died in their apartment. It seemed like a good time to split. So Duke and Jill packed their stuff and moved east, to Avenue D.

They decided to have a party to celebrate their new place. Duke bought a couple of six-packs and some bags of chips, and Jill made dip. Duke also borrowed some tapes from a buddy. Mostly Latin-type dance music. That was about it.

They put out the word, and maybe

twenty people showed up. Brought some bottles, and a generous amount of reefer. There wasn't much conversation, because, really, there wasn't much to talk about. Everyone just sat around getting loaded.

Jill's old boyfriend, Arnie, was there. He kept his eye on her and, when Duke disappeared into the next room with a young thing, they got together. The party got wild. Everyone took their clothes off. Jill took pictures.

Everyone agreed that they were having a really good time. So it was a real bummer when, later, the developed rolls of film got mailed to Jill's mother by mistake.

THE MURGATROYDS
LEAVE TOWN

DUKE WAS BACK ON THE STREET AGAIN, dealing to pay the rent. He had a pretty good connection—no money up front. But Duke would push his nickels and dimes, and then blow his profits on coke. He couldn't seem to get ahead. And the neighborhood was getting hot. The cops were having a field day out there. He knew all sorts of people on the block who'd been busted.

Jill, as usual, came up with the solution. "Why not make one really big buy," she said, "a really big buy, and I don't mean reefer either, and then chill out for a while. Maybe take a trip."

So Duke hit his connection for twenty thousand dollars' worth of cocaine. "I've got to get out of this grind," he told the man. The man nodded sympathetically and put his arm around Duke's shoulder. "Good luck," he said tenderly. "You know you're like a son to me. Just don't fuck this one up." He squeezed Duke's arm. A little too hard.

Duke took the stuff home and dumped it on the kitchen table. Jill seemed to have a little trouble comprehending the size and shape of it at first. Then she started jumping up and down.

"Let's celebrate," she said.

"Okay," Duke said, "but we can only do a little."

Jill (the name Murgatroyd hardly seemed to suit her) finished a second, then a third line.

"Honey, are you sure nobody followed you home?" she asked Duke.

"I don't think so," he replied, polishing off his fifth. "Though there was a strange dude hanging out on the corner," he said, frowning.

Jill crawled over to the window and peeked out.

"I see him, Duke, he's down there. The cops must have set you up. We'll be thrown in jail. I don't want to go to jail for the rest of my life," she wailed.

One thing led to another, and before either of them realized what they were doing the cocaine had been flushed down the toilet. Jill crawled back to the window. The man on the corner had left.

Knowing that they'd never be able to pay back the man, and that a low-level contract would be taken out on Duke (broken knees, fingers, etc), they decided to flee.

"We'll have to change our names," said Duke. "Maybe to Smith or something like that."

Thank God, thought Jill.

Daniel Kolm

DUKE & JILL BOTTOM-OUT

THEY MADE IT ALMOST TO the Ohio state border on Interstate 80 before their car broke down completely. It took them a couple of days to hitch back to the city. A friend let them crash in a tiny unused storeroom in the basement of a six-floor walkup.

Duke was feeling pretty discouraged by then. He had no money, no job, and no prospects of getting either in the near future.

Jill rallied and got a gig doing phone sales two days a week for a novelty company. She even figured out a way to get enough cash to get them through the week. She applied for an American Express Card and got her boss to lie about her salary. She'd call around, using the phone at work, and find out which of her friends were about to go on a shopping spree—go to the store with them on her days off and charge their purchases on her card— and then get the cash later. Of course a scheme like that could only last so long. She was beginning to approach her credit limit.

Duke pitched in with a couple of ideas of his own. He collected beer bottles and soda cans from city trash baskets, and panhandled on the street. And every afternoon he'd sit on a worn blanket outside the Cooper Union Building and try to sell off the last of their possessions—his old platform shoes, Jill's beat-up spikes, some tattered paperbacks and a couple of well-thumbed through girlie magazines. He felt like a person from another era—like a ghost from the depression years—he'd seen pictures of them in the school library before he dropped out.

Duke kept hoping they'd be able to put together enough cash to swing another drug deal. But, realistically, he knew he'd have to figure out something else. The word was out, and no one in their right mind would take a chance on selling him anything. Someone was after them. Every day at noon a gray Mercedes would pull up in front of their building and sit there for half an hour or so, and then slowly drive away.

Jill was scared. She couldn't understand why Duke was treating the situation so lightly. But Duke had finally come up with a plan.

He made up a flyer announcing the availability of their space for sublet, and notched a row of tear slips with the telephone number of a pay-phone near his afternoon selling spot on the bottom. He xeroxed about fifty copies and posted them in health-food stores, coffee shops and in the neighborhood bookstore on St. Mark's Place. The response was immediate.

He ended up getting one month's rent and security from seven different people. They all seemed very happy to give him their money—and Duke was equally happy to receive it.

"Let's go get stoned," he said to Jill, as they walked west on East Fourth Street.

DUKE MAKES THE ART SCENE

DUKE WAS BEGINNING TO FEEL OUT OF IT walking around in his own neighborhood. It seemed as if most of the people he passed on the street had more money than he did—everyone was wearing expensive costumes and doing strange things with their hair. The junkies he'd known from years ago were all drifting away—and there were fancy new restaurants springing up all over the place.

Duke figured he'd better come up with some sort of career while there was still time. He didn't want to end up like the sunbaked winos who slept on the sidewalk. So he put his mind to work.

One night, while cadging a bunch of free drinks at an art gallery opening, it came to him. A plastic-coated sheet listing the prices of the paintings was lying on a table and Duke noticed the amounts with astonishment.

"Holy shit," he said out loud, "I could do better stuff than this."

He read up on the subject in a special issue of the *East Village Eye* which he 'borrowed' from the Gem Spa. Duke also 'borrowed' a candy bar at the same time. One article said that a well-known graffiti artist, some guy named Keith Haring, was tucking away quite a bundle, so Duke decided to head in that direction. He 'borrowed' a can of white spray paint from a hardware store and hopped a turnstile at the 8th Street subway stop.

"Pay your fare!" the token booth clerk yelled at him.

Duke walked along the platform till he found an unused ad space covered with black paper. He started to draw some stick figures doing exotic things to each other, only to be rudely interrupted by a big hand on his shoulder.

"Get outta here before I shove that can up your can," a cop snarled at him.

Having read about what the cops did to another graffiti artist, a dude named Michael Stewart, in that same issue of the *Eye*, Duke didn't stick around to argue the point. He split at great speed, his hopes of making an instant fortune in the art world evaporating.

The next day, on the way to his usual selling spot near the Cooper Union Building, he came across a broken generator armature in a dumpster. It looked like an interesting piece of junk, so he took it along.

He carefully arranged his stuff on a

worn blanket, displaying each item to its best advantage, and then sat back to examine his new find. The afternoon dragged by. A couple of rowdy NYU kids laughed at the used lingerie and spiked high heels he was trying to sell. Duke was bored. He sat in the sun idly fooling around with the armature. He attached it to a splintered piece of pegboard and signed his name on it with the white spray paint. He tossed the result aside and sat back on his blanket, tired and disgusted with the world.

About five minutes later a limo driving by stopped abruptly and a trendy-looking fellow leaped out and rushed over towards Duke's spot.

"I must have that piece for my collection," he cried. He scooped up the mounted armature and asked Duke how much it cost.

"Five hundred bucks," Duke replied coolly, not batting an eye.

JILL GETS FASHIONABLE

JILL WAS TIRED OF BEING CALLED A
HIPPIE by the punks on St. Mark's Place.
Her shag had long since grown out and
lost its shape, and her jeans had patches
on the patches. She felt totally out of it.
And worse, she was beginning to feel
old.

Damn, she thought, I'd better take
some steps fast, or Duke's gonna start
looking around.

She wandered into a neighborhood
bar to think things over and have a
drink or two. She only intended to have
a couple of beers. Jill was trying to save

money. She'd been laid-off from her job at the novelty company. And she only had seventy-five dollars left of her severance pay.

Many drinks later, she made up her mind. She'd do a complete makeover! And with her courage fortified by a large dose of alcohol she stumbled across 7th Street towards the Astor Place Hair-cutters.

"What'll it be, Miss?" the barber asked her.

"I don't know," she slurred. "I want to change my look."

"Well, we do a lot of Madonnas," he said.

"Nah, gimmie a Mohawk ... and color it blue. 1 feel blue and I want my hairs to match." A short time later she stood outside on Astor Place, a cool breeze playing on parts of her head she never knew existed before. Startled commuters on their way home from work stared at her. She felt good. It was nice to be noticed.

Next she went into a cheap boutique and bought a second-hand pair of black pants. A size too small. She dumped her old jeans in a wastebasket by the dressing room door. She also bought a black leather vest. It wiped out the last of her cash, but it had the neatest silver studs on the shoulders.

She had to go back to their tiny apartment to put on the final touch. "I know exactly what I've got to do," she said out loud. "Duke will be so proud of me!" She took a half-finished bottle of whiskey from behind a stack of dirty dishes and polished it off. Then she took some ice cubes and a needle to the bathroom with her.

Leaning on the sink, she looked at herself in the mirror. It took a couple of moments to bring her reflection into focus. Then she quickly punched three holes in each side of her nose and inserted three different pairs of earrings. There was blood all over the place—tiny streams of red stained the sink—and droplets splattered onto the tiled floor.

***

Jill walked back over to Avenue A. There was a gaggle of punks hanging out in front of the Pyramid Club. Jill joined them. Nobody said a word.

She'd been accepted.

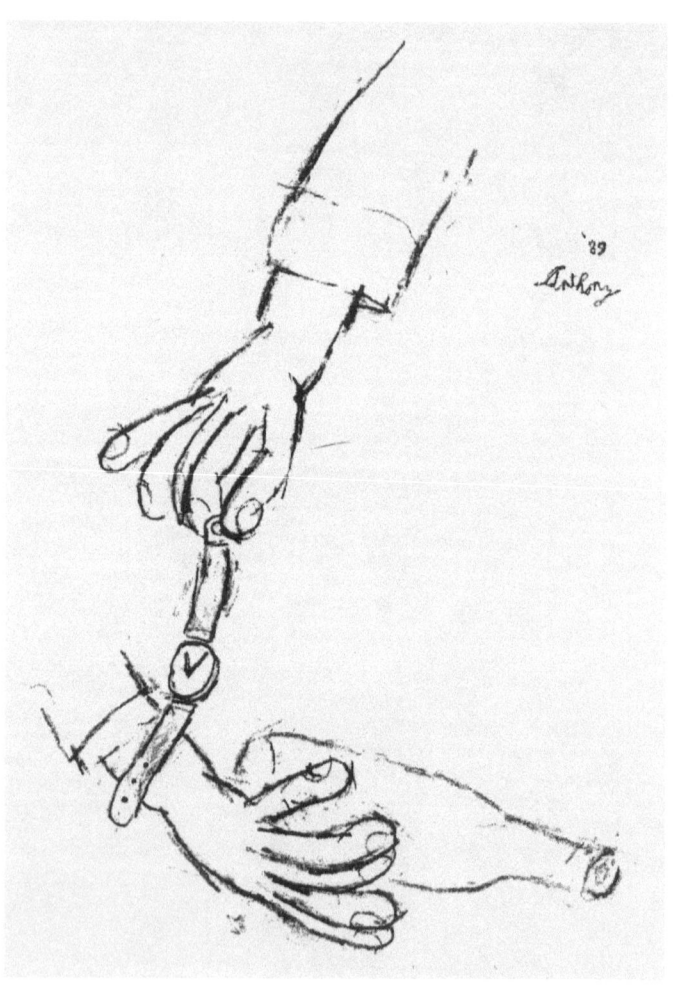

Bill Anthony

THE ANARCHIST
NEW YEAR'S EVE PARTY

IT WAS GOING TO BE A LONELY NEW YEAR'S EVE for Duke. Jill had to visit her mom in the hospital—and Duke hadn't planned ahead. He usually spent New Year's Eve in a neighborhood bar with Jill, getting totally ripped. In fact, last year he managed to get them thrown out of three different places. Before midnight.

Duke rolled a joint and left their apartment in a bad mood. He headed towards his favorite bar on Avenue A— only to find it closed. Boarded up by the city.

"Fucking shit," he muttered, his words forming clouds in the cold air. "What am I gonna do now?"

He circled the block a couple of times trying to figure out where to go. He finally went inside a bookstore on St. Mark's Place to get warm. A bulletin board cluttered with flyers caught his eye. Looking through them he came across a small card inviting everyone to an Anarchist New Year's Eve Party. It sounded pretty strange. But there would probably be free booze. So Duke decided to check it out. He ripped the announcement off the wall and stuffed it in his pocket.

It took him awhile to find a building to match the address on the torn card. It was past Avenue C on a block where most of the tenements were either abandoned or destroyed by fire. Piles of charred bricks only partially covered by snow lined the broken sidewalks.

I wonder if anarchists do drugs, Duke thought. He banged on the door. Someone opened it and told him to come in.

Inside was like another world. A bunch of people clustered around a kerosene heater were arguing loudly. One guy kept jabbing everyone in the chest with his index finger to emphasize what he was saying, but they seemed to be having a good time. Duke edged past them and sat down on the floor next to a sagging sofa. He wanted to take his time and ease into this one.

A dude on the sofa turned to him and said, "Hi, *my* name is Vern. I'm an anarchist *and* a survivalist. *I'm* going to make it through the next war. I've got this concussion-proof watch with a built-in compass, and I've got an escape route out of the city *all mapped out.* I won't get trapped here like a *dumb hippie.*"

"Good for you," Duke said. He mentally tried to calculate how much coke the watch would buy.

A woman sitting next to Vern leaned over and told Duke her name was Kat and that she'd come to the party with this guy and, really, he wasn't much fun and, hey, she had this cute little tattoo of a butterfly on the inside of her thigh and would he be interested in joining her in the next room for a closer look?

"Sure," Duke said. "Are you an anarchist, too?"

"Of course," Kat replied. "Isn't everyone?"

***

Hours later, trying to find the door, Duke stumbled over a body surrounded by empty bottles. It was Vern, passed out on the floor.

Duke bent over him and slipped the watch off his wrist.

"Thanks, buddy," he said softly, putting it in his pocket. "Happy New Year."

Shalom Neuman

A BAD DAY

DUKE KNEW IT WAS GOING TO BE A BAD DAY, even before he got out of bed. He had a splitting headache, and a lump the size of a nickel bag on the back of his neck. He couldn't remember where he'd been last night—or how he got home. Jill was nowhere around. She'd probably gone out to look for another part-time job.

Duke dragged himself into their tiny kitchen to get a bite to eat. But of course there wasn't a single bit of food in the house—which shouldn't have surprised him—there seldom was.

"Fucking shit," he groaned, "now I'm gonna have to go out."

He took the bike he'd 'borrowed' from a friend down six flights of steps to the street. He was sweating and cursing by the time he finally reached the ground floor. Duke aimed himself towards one of the cheap Ukrainian coffee shops in the neighborhood and pedaled off. A bit unsteadily.

About five blocks from his building he smacked into a pothole. He saw it at the last moment and tried to swerve around it but a speeding *New York Post* delivery truck didn't give him any choice. He broke a couple of spokes and bent the front tire.

"Fucking shit!" he yelled. He righted the bike and started to walk it in the direction of the restaurant.

"Well, my friend," a guy in an army jacket said to him, "looks like you've got problems."

"Yeah," Duke mumbled, noticing that the guy had one hand stuck inside a brown paper bag.

"I'd like to use your wheels for a while," the guy said.

"Go fuck yourself," Duke replied.

"Hey, be cool, man. I got a gun in this here sack," the guy said, grinning. He gave Duke a flash of metal. "And I want your cash, too."

"It's yours," Duke said quickly, letting go of the bike.

The guy took his money and told him to split. Duke went back to his building, his stomach growling. He'd have to get some stuff to sell on the street to get some cash so he could eat. What a lousy day.

But it got worse. He got back just in time to see through a newly smashed door two guys ducking out a window with the few things of any value they had left. Duke was too wasted to give chase.

***

It took him a couple of hours to panhandle enough money to buy a new lock for the door and a sandwich. As he entered his building again a voice called out from behind the stairwell:

"Stick 'em up."

"Fucking *shit!*" Duke said. "I don't *have* anything. We just *got* robbed."

"What's in the bag?" the voice asked.

"A new lock for our apartment and a sandwich," Duke replied.

"That'll do just fine," the voice said. "Hand it over."

"Can I at least keep the *sandwich*?" Duke asked.

"No," the voice answered.

Bill Anthony

BAD KARMA

IT WAS HAZY, HOT AND HUMID. Gritty summer air banged down on the tarpaper roof of the abandoned building on Avenue C where Duke and Jill lived, bringing the temperature inside to a slow boil. Duke was crouched in a corner of their room, surrounded by stacks of porno mags, water-damaged books, and heaps of women's clothing.

"Watcha doin,' honey?" Jill asked him.

"Taking inventory," he growled back. Duke was in a bad mood. The heat was making him sweat heavily, and drops of it were falling onto his best magazines—the ones he'd managed to keep in mint condition despite the daily grind of trying to sell them on the street.

"Fucking shit!" Duke cursed, wiping his face with a lacy pink nighty. "Damn it, Jill, our stock is running really low—we don't have enough good stuff left to get us more than a six-pack or two, and maybe a nickel bag."

"I get the message," Jill yelled from the sweltering bathroom. She was trying to mousse her grown-out shag into a bouffant. "You want me to go out and cop some merchandise."

"Yeah," Duke said. "What I really need are more 'zines—these are getting too fucking beat up."

Jill rummaged through the piles of dirty clothing for a pair of large-waisted jeans with sharply tapered legs. She also put on a loose black T-shirt and left it untucked.

"You know how much I hate doing this," she said to Duke. She chugged down a couple of beers. Then she did a few lines to give her an edge and left the tiny hot apartment.

The streets were steaming.

Jill checked out Gem Spa and the other neighborhood newsstands, but they were all on to her. With "get the the fuck oudda here, ya thief" still ringing in her ears, Jill sat down on the curb and popped some pills to help her think. Unfortunately, the only idea she could come up with was to steal some product from another peddler.

Jill lurched over to the large black cube sculpture at the triangular intersection of Fourth Avenue and Lafayette Street. A bunch of street peddlers were set up there, displaying their wares in the shadow of the cube. One guy was selling bootleg Dead tapes, another featured several plastic milk crates filled with badly scratched jazz LPs.

Jill felt dizzy. The heat seemed to be magnifying the effects of the pills as she scanned the various items for sale. She leaned on the sculpture for support. And then, swimming into focus, there they were—row upon row of vintage soft-core porn magazines—*Swank*, *Genesis*, *Penthouse*, *High Society*, *Hustler* and yes, a 1953 *Playboy* —all of them in perfect condition. Just what Duke wanted.

Jill got it together and approached the sun-baked, pot-bellied man who sat smiling amid them. He was wearing only a tattered pair of cutoffs and his bald head gleamed in the sun.

"Can you tell me where St. Mark's Place is?" she slurred.

The man looked beatifically into her wildly gyrating green eyes. As he turned to point out directions she scooped up an armful of magazines, slid them under her shirt and skillfully tucked them into the top of her jeans in one fluid motion. And that's when the heat, the beers and the drugs hit her full force. She fell face down on the concrete.

At that exact moment Duke showed up—he'd gone out to score some stuff on his own. He sprinted over to Jill, rolled her onto her back and put his head against her chest to check for a heartbeat. As he did so, the spine of a porno mag poked him in the eye through her T-shirt.

Thinking quickly, Duke hoisted Jill up by the armpits and draped her over his shoulder in such a way as to keep the stolen booty from shaking loose and falling out.

"Hey, man," Duke said to the peddler, "too much to drink—happens all the time—I'll see that she gets home okay." Duke grinned at the man in fraternal understanding and then staggered off under the dead weight of Jill's limp body.

***

Darkness brought no relief—if anything, the humidity seemed to increase, and a thick dirty fog settled over the Lower East Side.

Duke arranged his display of girlie magazines on a flattened piece of cardboard in front of 'Love Saves the Day,' the hip chotchke shop on the corner of 7th Street and 2nd Avenue. He carefully positioned his newest treasure, the 1953 *Playboy*, in the center of it. Jill had scored really big this time. He'd carried her all the way back to their joint, his tank top rank with sweat. After dragging her up five flights of stairs, he was finally able to revive her.

Duke snapped back to reality—a guy had picked up his centerpiece and was thumbing through the pages. Duke checked him out. He was a large, muscular white guy, dressed all in black; black pants, black leather jacket and black motorcycle boots. Guy must be crazy, Duke thought, it's still fuckin' 90 degrees! The guy's greasy 50s-style pompadour contrasted sharply with Duke's stringy shoulder-length hair.

The guy casually rolled up the *Playboy*, jammed it in his jacket pocket and turned away, walking north towards St. Marks Place.

"Hey, fucking shit, man—that's my merchandise!" Duke yelled. "Ya gotta pay for it if you want it!" The guy didn't stop. "Hey, man, watch my stuff—I'll be right back," Duke said to the peddler selling next to him. He jumped up and ran after the guy, who made no attempt to get away.

The big guy walked nonchalantly up 2nd Avenue, seemingly oblivious to Duke's shouting and cursing. He turned east, crossing the avenue at 9th Street, and Duke followed. He was livid with anger, but he didn't know what to do. The guy was way too big to attack— Duke was a skinny five-foot-six, even Jill towered over him—he didn't really want to die over a magazine—and he couldn't very well call for the cops—they'd probably bust him, too.

As they neared the middle of the block the guy whirled around, his jacket fanning out, and he whipped his hand towards Duke as if he had a weapon in it. Duke jumped back, startled. But the guy merely gave him a weird smile and continued along 9th Street to 1st Avenue.

Duke was perplexed, and more than a little shaken up, but he stayed right on the guy's tail—just far enough back to run if the guy tried to charge him again.

They reached 1st Avenue, crossed it, and turned uptown towards 10th Street. And it was at that corner, in front of a neighborhood bodega, where the big guy made his final move. He stopped abruptly, picked up a heavy steel trash basket filled with garbage and heaved it at Duke. Duke just barely managed to avoid it. At that moment he noticed a long line of large green trash bags on the sidewalk, and a tiredness filled him as he pictured himself having to dodge each and every one of them.

The guy came at Duke shouting, "What do you want from me, faggot? You want to suck my ass? Is that it, faggot, you want to suck my ass?"

Duke looked around in desperation for any kind of weapon—and saw what appeared to be a stick protruding from one of the garbage bags. Duke pulled it out and was surprised to find himself holding a four-foot long broken fluorescent light tube with a jagged end. Fucking shit, I'm Obi-wan Kenobi, he thought.

"Yo, my man, don't hit him with that thing," someone said, "You'll get little slivers of glass in our eyes."

Duke looked over and saw a giant black dude with sweat bands on his wrists. And then it hit Duke—this was a drug corner, and that dude was the Main Man—and he and his new 'friend' were disturbing the evening's commerce—their fracas might even rouse the cops—and the black dude obviously didn't want that to happen.

"S'up, my man," the Dealer asked Duke.

"Hey, man, I sell on the street, just like you, and that guy took something that belongs to me," he answered.

"Give it up," the black dude ordered the white guy, which he quickly did, meekly handing the *Playboy* back to Duke, then splitting. "Now you go back to your spot and be cool with the tube —you don't want to be getting little slivers of glass in your eyes." And he flashed Duke the peace sign.

Under a streetlight on 9th Street Duke looked down at the cover of the *Playboy*, savoring the sexy pose of the girl who adorned it. She was once again his. But, damn, several droplets of water stitched a pattern across her body. Was his sweat ruining yet another magazine? Duke wiped his forehead with the back of his free hand—and it was then that he heard a long dull rumble of violent summer thunder.

Duke looked up just as the heavens opened.

Gregory Kolm

HOOK

"WHAT THE FUCK!" DUKE MUTTERED, amazed at what he was seeing in the darkened bookstore. A thin curtain of smoke was rising from under the baseboard like an inverted waterfall. It stretched the entire length of the left wall.

Holy shit, the joint's on fire! I better get the fuck out of here, he thought, turning back towards the bathroom window he'd just busted to get in. But then he noticed something odd—the smoke smelled like marijuana—one of his favorite things—so he hesitated a moment—and then he became aware of the pounding and shaking—it felt like a humongous semi grinding down St. Mark's Place in second gear.

And, finally, he picked up on the sounds; shouting, cursing, music (Duke had problems with his hearing—way too much heavy metal over the years).

"Jesus, must be some kinda weird party or something goin' on next door," Duke said, thinking out loud while lighting a stray joint he found in his pocket. He was curious and, anyway, he could always come back later to clean the place out—so Duke hoisted himself through the splintered window frame and dropped down onto the bare plot of ground behind the bookstore.

The space next to the East Village Bookstore had been converted into a unisex haircutting boutique: HAIRPOWER TO THE PEOPLE. It had a couple of windows in the rear wall, so Duke eased over to check things out.

"Man, world's totally fuckin' nuts!" he whistled. All the furniture had been piled against the walls and the front grates had been lowered. Bathed in unnaturally bright light, a bunch of Hell's Angels, dressed in full colors, were slow-dancing with the male hairdressers.

One of the Angels seemed to be holding a metallic object; light glinted on it brightly. Duke squinted, trying to determine if it was a gun or a knife— but it turned out to be neither. This particular Angel had a mechanical hook for a hand and, in thrall to the music, he pressed it deeply into the small of his partner's back.

Now Duke remembered. He'd seen this guy hanging out on St. Mark's Place, hassling passing tourists. The Angel would use his hook as bait, attracting the naive, the curious and the stupid, engage them in conversation, turn it strange, get pissed off and then beat the unsuspecting victim to a pulp with his steely contraption.

Duke winced—not his idea of a good time. He turned to re-enter the bookstore just as the music changed. The slow song segued into the raucous chords of the Dead Kennedys' '*Too Drunk to Fuck*', and the partygoers began to slam into each other like battered cars in a demolition derby.

Duke couldn't help himself—he started pogoing spastically—and that was his undoing. One of the Angels noticed his pale countenance bobbing up and down outside the window. He let out a yell, directing all eyes towards the back of the barbershop. Everyone froze—and then, as if at a hidden command, an angry horde of sweaty, drug-crazed psychopaths charged the back door.

Duke frantically jumped at a fire escape ladder dangling just above his head and managed to grab hold of the bottom rung. He pulled his skinny, drug-wasted body up by sheer will alone. The Angel with the hook took a swipe at Duke's disappearing leg, snagging a strip of already frayed jeans.

***

The hot, noonday sun beat down on a frazzled Duke. He was squatting against the blue, cinderblock wall of the St. Mark's Cinema, very broke and totally stoned. Somehow he was gonna have to figure out another way to rip off the bookstore across the street—man, there was only one fucking clerk running the whole joint—that's practically an open invitation—shit, hitting a place like that should be as easy as taking a crap.

Doing the bathroom window again at night was flat out. Earlier in the day he'd seen a couple of repair guys with toolboxes and armloads of two-by-fours go into the shop, followed by a lot of hammering and drilling.

Armed robbery was also out of the question—the cops had confiscated his gun—something about one of his friends getting blown away while playing Russian roulette with it.

Duke decided on the direct approach. He got up, crossed the street and stepped into the dank, ill-lit recesses of the bookstore. Books and pamphlets were casually strewn around on old wooden sale tables. Duke checked out the guy working at the front counter; a tall, long-haired dude with thick John Lennon granny glasses. The clerk seemed to be deeply engrossed in an underground comic—*Zap #4*, Duke guessed from the cover.

This'll be like taking candy from a fuckin' baby, he thought, walking back towards the very bathroom he'd broken into last night. To the right of the bathroom was a small messy office, created by running mass-market display racks out from the wall. Duke sidled in behind the makeshift barrier.

Inside, a half-eaten sandwich adorned a chipped wooden desk, next to tumbled stacks of indecipherable ledgers. A battered bicycle was chained to one of the legs. Duke simply tilted the desk back and slipped the lock free. Yeah, he'd take the bike—it had real value—not like those fucking books—you had to heist so many of them to make it worth your while.

He rummaged through the desk looking for cash, but came up empty. Duke shrugged, stuffed the sandwich in his pocket and wheeled the bike towards the exit.

Just as he was about to leave the premises, the bookstore clerk materialized in front of him—from out of thin air—blocking his path.

"Hey, man, what do you think you're doing? That doesn't belong to you. Please be cool and put it back," the apparition lectured. It was dressed in a faded tie-dyed T-shirt and ancient bell bottoms. For sure this one don't live on the street, Duke thought.

"I really must ask you to split, or I'll be forced to call the police," the obstruction continued, grabbing the handlebars and attempting to wrest the bike from Duke.

That was a mistake. Duke popped the guy, knocking him to the floor.

"Get the fuck out of my way, asshole —I hate old hippies," Duke snarled, pushing the bicycle out of the store. He looked back to see if the clerk was going to try to get up and follow him, and felt the bike bump into something —or someone. Duke whirled around and found himself face to face with the one-armed Angel (the tourist he'd been messing with gladly fled).

"I remember you," the Angel gloated, raising his hook.

NATURAL ENEMIES

I WAS WALKING DOWN ST. MARK'S PLACE, looking for someone to hang out with, when I ran into Duke. He was sitting on the blue painted steps in front of the old Electric Circus, a can of beer in each hand.

"Hey, man, how's it hangin'?" I asked.

"Not too fucking bad," he snickered, waving his beers at a couple of Alcoholics Anonymous who'd just stepped out of their meeting to grab a smoke. "I'm buggin' the shit out of them—cracks me up, man."

The AA guys ducked and ran back inside.

"Fucking pussies," he said. "Hey, let's go get some beers at Little Peter's."

"Okay," I said, "but I don't want to mess with the girls. Just have a beer...that's all."

Little Peter's was a sleazy topless joint on the corner of 2nd Avenue and 5th Street. You could do almost anything there for a five spot except fuck.

***

The first girl to start down the line still seemed to like men. She'd look at the ceiling and make a trilling noise when the guys did stuff to her. Then she'd tuck the bill in her G-string and move on to the next customer. When she reached us, we passed.

I bought us some beers—Duke was broke.

The next girl was a thin brunette with a piercing look that said she knew about men and sex and power, and she wasn't having any of it. She didn't even want to take off her top, but the bouncer told her to be cool.

"Let's get out of here," I said to Duke. "This one's too fucking weird."

"No, man, I'm getting turned-on," he said. "Loan me a five."

When she got to our end of the bar, 1 passed. She crawled over me and squatted on Duke's lap. He got very animated, and started doing all sorts of tricky things to her with his hands and fingers and tongue. Duke was putting his coolest moves on display for everyone in the bar.

He finished and pulled away from her with a smirk.

"How much you gonna' charge me?" he said, probably thinking she'd say, 'Nothing, honey. This one's on me.'

But instead, she stared at him coldly and hissed, "For jerks like you it's double—ten bucks!"

Bill Anthony

NOTES TO MYSELF

SPRING HAD FINALLY COME AGAIN to the East Village. And since it was spring, it was time for Duke to get off his tired ass and peddle some stuff. There wasn't anyone who was going to give him free food and rent these days, 'cause times had changed. Now the cops were manfully busting anyone who set up shop on the street, tossing confiscated merchandise into vans, then disappearing it forever into the endless labyrinth of the criminal justice system.

Duke wandered around the neighborhood wondering what he could move besides drugs. Drugs had

gotten him into a shit-load of trouble—
Duke had a rap sheet two inches thick
—he'd even gotten smacked on the head
by a SWAT cop as he walked by
Tompkins Square Park late one night,
stoned, speaking his mind just like
Michael Carter had done, with the
same result—another bust and he'd be
doing hard time for sure.

As he walked across St. Mark's Place
he noticed one group of street vendors
that wasn't being hassled by the pigs—
the guys selling books on folding tables.
So Duke sidled up to a bearded gent
and asked him why he was able to
operate without interference.

"Because we're protected by the
First Amendment, comrade," he was
told.

"What's that fuckin' mean, asshole
—don't mess with my head," Duke
hissed menacingly.

"See, the First Amendment protects
free speech," the guy said, ignoring the
attitude Duke was giving him, "and

books are part of that process—the unobstructed transmission and exchange cf information."

"So the cops can't fuck with you?" Duke asked.

"That's putting it baldly, but yes," the old-timer answered, as he took a couple of dollars from a student type for a battered paperback. *Beneath the Empire of the Birds*, the cover read. I got to cut myself into this racket, Duke said to himself, and off he went to look for stock.

Duke knew he couldn't steal the stuff, for the same reason he couldn't deal drugs. Unfortunately, Jill wouldn't be able to help this time. She'd ditched him on account of poverty and was now living in a studio apartment in the garment district. Not having any light in the tiny bathroom they shared in the hall with the other squatters had been the last straw. Somebody'd recently told Duke that Jill was dancing at Billy's

Topless to get together enough dough to go to F.I.T.

Duke went to the dumpster behind his neighborhood Barnes and Noble and filled a couple of shopping bags with damaged paperbacks. He was kinda stumped as to why all the books were missing covers. Must be a fashion statement of some sort or another, he figured. He lined up the stripped mass markets in several neat rows on a dirty green blanket on 2nd Avenue and then sat back to await his first customer.

The nattily attired yuppies who streamed by looked at him as if he were dung, moving to the other side of the walk, avoiding any eye contact.

"Assholes," Duke growled.

Time slowed to a crawl. Duke flipped through the books arrayed before him, but the print was too small in most of them for his bleary drug-addled eyes. But hey, hold on, one of them did have large print, and a lot of space between each sentence as well.

"Okay," Duke said, "let's give this fucker a shot!"

The first sentence read:

> If I had only . . .
> forgotten future greatness
> and looked at the green things
> and the buildings
> and reached out to those around me
> and smelled the air
> and ignored the forms
> and the self-styled obligations
> and heard the rain on the roof
> and put my arms around my wife

"Fucking shit," Duke muttered, "guess I do still miss Jill." And then:

> What an absurd amount of energy I have been wasting all my life trying to figure out how things "really are" when all the time they weren't

... and ...

God revealed his name to
Moses, and it was I AM
WHAT I AM

Jesus, isn't that what Popeye used to
say, he mused. Duke read on:

When I can get where I can
enjoy just lying on the rug
and picking up lint balls, I
will no longer be too
ambitious

Right on! he agreed. And even better,
there was stuff about drugs:

The rainbow is more beautiful
than the pot at the end of it,
because the rainbow is now.
And the pot never turns out to
be quite what I expected.

Bummer, Duke sympathized. He took a
handful of pills from his pocket and
popped them in his mouth. This stuff is
deep, he thought, got to clear my mind.

I live from one tentative
conclusion to the next,
thinking each one is final.
The only thing I know for
sure is that I'm confused.

. . . and finally . . .

Now that I know I'm no wiser
than anyone else, does this
wisdom make me wiser?

Duke sat there, bathed in tranquility,
and thus he had no real need for the
last sentence in the book which reads:

But the world is round, and a
messy mortal is my friend.
Come walk with me in the mud.

He shuddered slightly, and his soul
shook itself free and drifted out of his
sitting body and rose up high over the
Lower East Side and from that vantage
looked down at the coffee shops and

trendy restaurants and tourist hotels and expensive co-ops and pricey boutiques and yuppies on bikes and cops, cops, cops everywhere; on horses, in cars, on foot, patrolling in clusters, ticketing, bullying, evicting the last remnants of a world that was once so familiar to Duke, a world of danger and freedom, a world he'd watched evaporate, and his soul moved on, looking for Billy's Topless and, hopefully, Jill.

FOR ME WHAT CHANGED MY LIFE WAS VIETNAM – I HAD DEFINITELY MADE UP MY MIND THAT I WAS NOT GOING TO GET IN A POSITION TO SHOOT ANYONE OR KILL ANYONE – SO I VOLUNTEERED FOR ALTERNATIVE SERVICE & GOT SENT TO APPALACHIA – IT WAS 1969 – THE WOMAN I WAS WITH AT THAT TIME & I GOT PLACED IN A SMALL COMMUNITY OF RUNDOWN TAR PAPER SHACKS – IT WAS CALLED MAURIN ROW – THIS COMMUNITY GOT ONLY COLD RUNNING WATER FROM THE CITY & NO SEWAGE OR GARBAGE PICK-UP – WE HAD AN OUTHOUSE & I KNEW I HAD MADE IT IN AN INTERESTING PLACE WHEN SNOWFLAKES FALLING BETWEEN THE WOOD SLATS LANDED & MELTED ON MY KNEES WHILE I WAS TAKING A DUMP – BECAUSE I WAS SUPPOSEDLY A 'COMMUNITY ORGANIZOR' IT WAS IMPOSSIBLE TO GET A STRAIGHT JOB WHEN I FINALLY MOVED TO NEW YORK CITY IN 1970 – THE ONLY WAY I COULD GET MONEY TO PAY THE RENT WAS TO SELL MY LIBRARY IN BITS & PIECES TO THE STRAND BOOKSTORE – EVERYTIME I WENT THERE FRED BASS, THE OWNER'S SON WOULD OFFER ME A JOB – THE STARTING SALARY WAS $60 GROSS A WEEK & YOU HAD TO WORK SATURDAYS SO I PUT OFF WORKING THERE AS LONG AS POSSIBLE UNTIL I FINALLY CAVED ON ACCOUNT OF HUNGER – AT THAT TIME I WAS LIVING IN A BASEMENT APARTMENT IN BROOKLYN THAT USED TO FLOOD EVERYTIME IT RAINED – AT THE STRAND I WORKED WITH PATTI SMITH, RICHARD HELL & TOM VERLAINE – I SAW TELEVISION THE FIRST NIGHT THEY PLAYED CBGB, WHEN RICHARD HELL WAS STILL IN THE BAND – I GOT FIRED FOR A STUPID REASON & ENDED UP GETTING A GIG AT THE EASTSIDE BOOKSTORE ON ST. MARKS PLACE AT 2ND AVE – THIS WOULD BE 1975 – IT WAS AN INTERESTING TIME – THE EAST VILL-

-AGE WAS KIND OF ON FIRE & WE WOULD WALK OUT OF THE BOOKSTORE & WATCH THE FIRE TRUCKS HEAD EAST – PEOPLE WOULD COME INTO THE BOOKSTORE & STEAL ANYTHING THAT WASN'T NAILED DOWN – ONE NIGHT I WAS IN THE STORE ALONE & THIS SMALL GUY COMES OUT OF THE OFFICE IN THE BACK WHEELING THE MANAGER'S BICYCLE TOWARDS THE FRONT DOOR – WHEN I TOLD HIM TO PUT IT BACK HE WALKED OVER TO THE REGISTER & STUCK A KNIFE INTO THE BACK OF MY HAND WHERE IT GOT STUCK SO HE HAD TO LET GO OF IT – HE WAS TOTALLY DRUNK & I COULD'VE KILLED HIM – I COULD'VE DONE ANYTHING I WANTED BUT IT WASN'T WORTH IT SO I JUST TOLD HIM TO SPLIT!

Fly

Ron Kolm is one of the founding members of the Unbearables literary collective, and an editor of several of their anthologies: *Crimes of the Beats*, *The Worst Book I Ever Read* and *The Unbearables Big Book of Sex!* Ron is a contributing editor of *Sensitive Skin* magazine and the editor of the *Evergreen Review*. He is the author of *The Plastic Factory* and the co-author, with Jim Feast, of the novel, *Neo Phobe*. A collection of his poems, *Divine Comedy*, was published by Fly By Night Press, and a new one, *Suburban Ambush*, came out from Autonomedia. He's had work published in *Live Mag!, Gathering of the Tribes, the Poetry Super Highway, Urban Graffiti, MungBeing* and *the Outlaw Bible of American Poetry*. Ron Kolm has worked in many of the signature independent bookstores of New York City over the years: The Strand, St. Mark's Bookshop, Shakespeare & Co, and currently, Posman Books. Kolm's papers were purchased by the New York University library, where they've been catalogued in the Fales Collection as part of the Downtown Writers Group.

OTHER TITLES FROM

UNKNOWN PRESS

IF I HAD WINGS THESE WINDMILLS
WOULD BE DEAD
CHUCK HOWE

Engaging, endearing, heartfelt. Also, full of the wild meandering song of youth, equal amounts of blood, drugs and music spilling out of everything, IF I HAD WINGS THESE WINDMILLS WOULD BE DEAD is Chuck Howe's debut collection of short fiction. It contains linked stories that carry the reader along in an addictive manner, starting from the beginning–following a young protagonist through all sorts of strange adventures. At times feeling like a literary Calvin and Hobbes tromping through mountain trails and backwoods pines, getting into all sorts of trouble, and later growing up into Hunter S. Thompson

STUDIES
WILLIAM SEWARD BONNIE

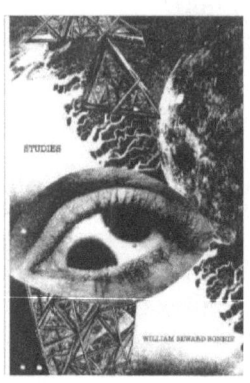

In "Studies," a new collection of poetry by William S. Bonnie, we are taken to the silent moments of a long distance relationship. Bonnie is a troubadour of the holy afterthought. Reading it is like wading quietly near the lip of an ocean, and on what appears to be a hundred poems about the same topic, we are reminded of the excessive amount of time we allow ourselves to intimately wander. In comparison to Bonnie's previous work, his latest effort has made a truce with brevity. Bonnie holds a fresh perspective with a knack for simple rhymes that do not feel forced but rather allow him to hone his stream of consciousness into tightly wound and seamless packages.

TOO MUCH

AN ANTHOLOGY ABOUT EXCESS

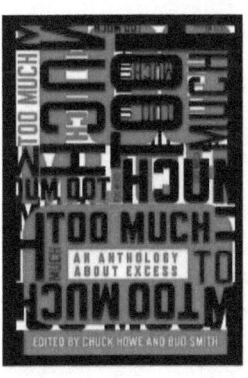

A diverse assemblage of writers lay down all there is to say about the time they went too far. *Too Much* features blistering accounts told from a wild array of perspectives and experiences: from trying to quit smoking to over-anxious internet misbehavior, eating disorders, sexual obsessions, drunken car rides through tropical hells and everything in between. Featuring contributions from Meg Tuite, Robert Vaughan, Ron Kolm, Chuck Howe, James Duncan, Misti Rainwater-Lites, Ashley Perez, and others.

FIRST TIME

AN ANTHOLOGY ABOUT LOST VIRGINITY

Four dozen writers retell the intimate details about how they lost their virgnity in this touching, hilarious and shocking collection. This enthralling assembly of short stories, essays, and poems never ceases to entertain. Everyone has a story about their first time, these writers take it to the limit, in this full length collection spanning 216 pages, complete with some illustrations from editor, Bud Smith. Contributors include: Nicole Adams, William Seward Bonnie, Mark Brunetti, Wolf Carstens, James Claffey, Marsha Calabro, Ryder Collins, Wanda Clevenger, Heather Dorn, Sam Garret, Mina Gorey, Lisa Hirsh, Chuck Howe, Chris Jamieson, Jason Neese Ashley Perez, Frank Reardon, Alex Reed, Paul Corman Roberts, Joe Saldibar, Meg Tuite, Robert Vaughan, Aaron Dietz, and more

THE PART TIME SHAMAN HANDBOOK
AN INTRODUCTION FOR BEGINNERS

MICHAEL GILAN MAXWELL

An instruction manual for those that cannot be taught. This pocket-sized collection of poems and incantations will guide you through all the bullshit and beyond. With lessons covering, The Edge, the Day-To-Day, Community, Finding Your Way, Principles For Living, Things To Do Before Going To Bed, Health, The Inner World and— everything you'll need to pack for your Vision Quest. Michael Gilan Maxwell is a master of self help *and* self destruction, who will lead you with bells and chants and Fritos covered in chili to find your way through roaring surf, and the chaos and fury of thunderstorms.

Forthcoming from
<small>UNKNOWN PRESS</small>

In Case We Die Anthology

Self Published Kindling:
Memoirs of a Homeless Bookstore Owner
Mik Everett

Things I Didn't Tell You
Stories
Erin Parker

+

Rift/Split
prose by
Robert Vaughan and Kathy Fish

www.unknowneverything.com

www.ingramcontent.com/pod-product-compliance
Lightning Source LLC
Chambersburg PA
CBHW050905180626
46814CB00007B/2901